ROGER'S HOT PANCAKES

£5.25

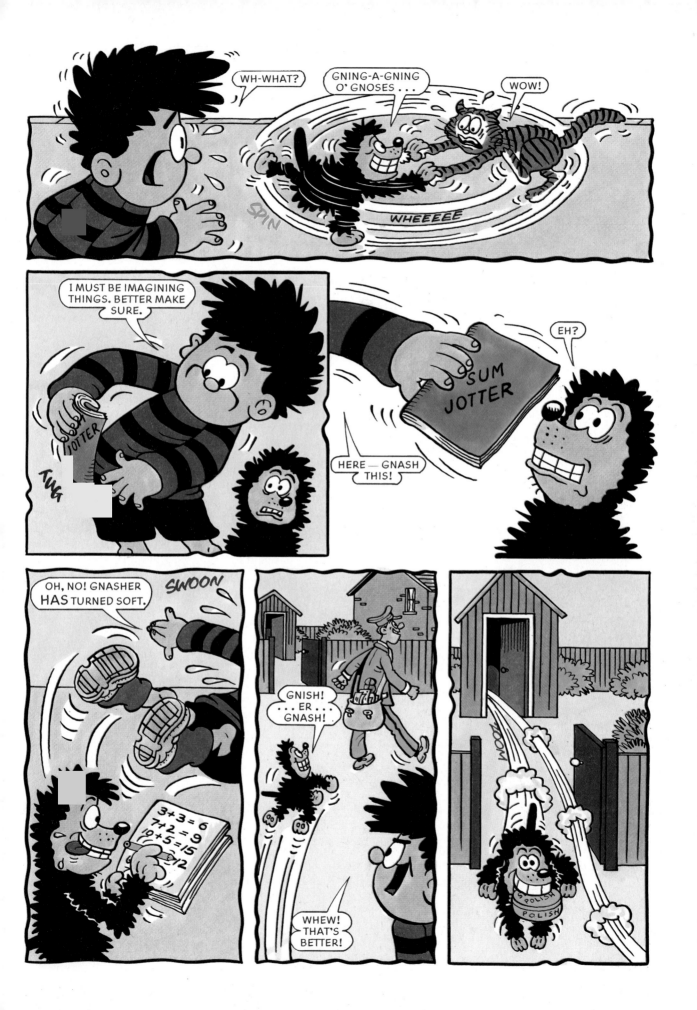

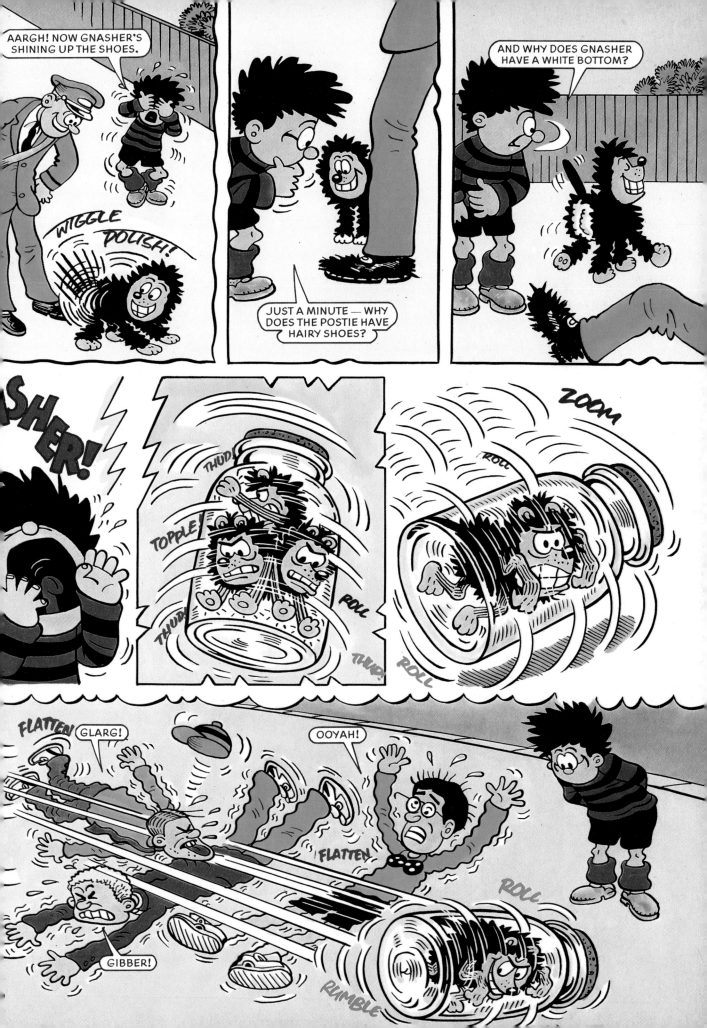

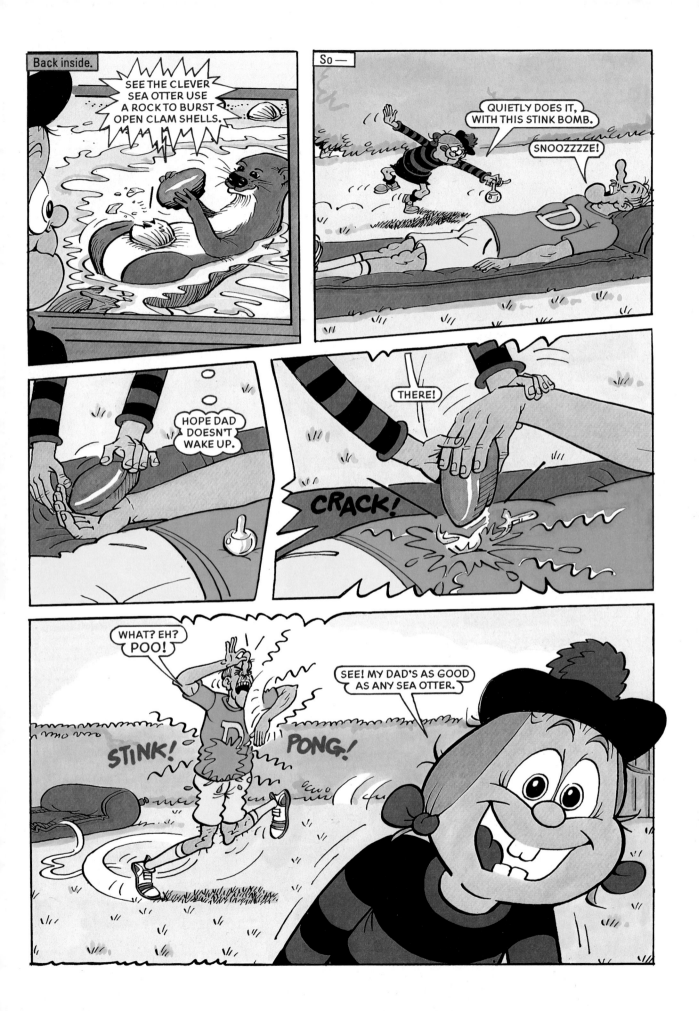

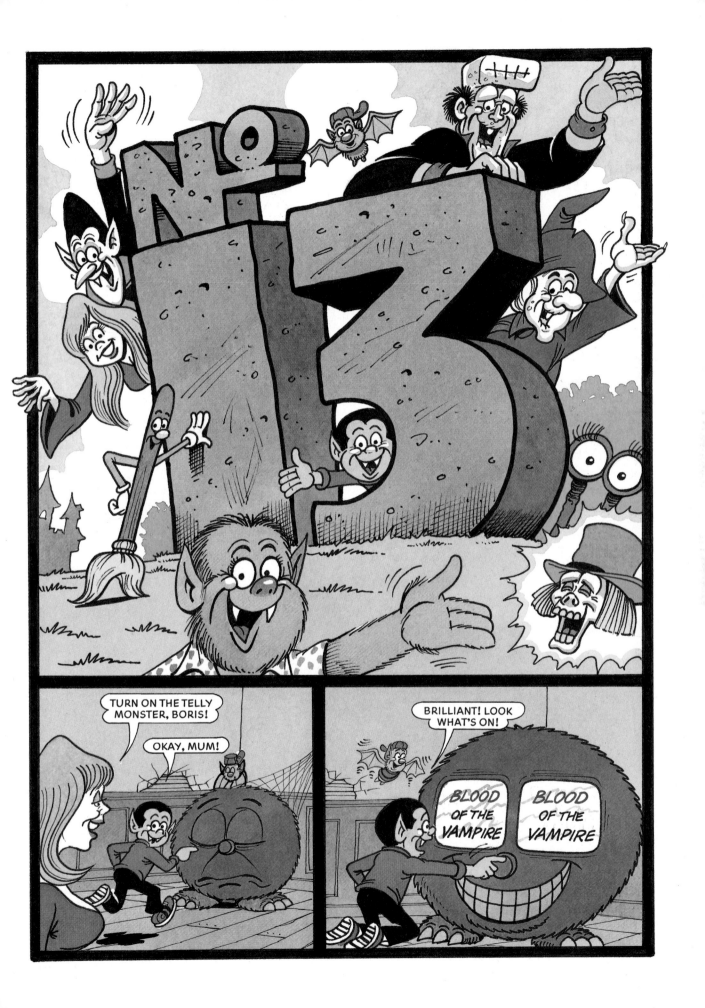

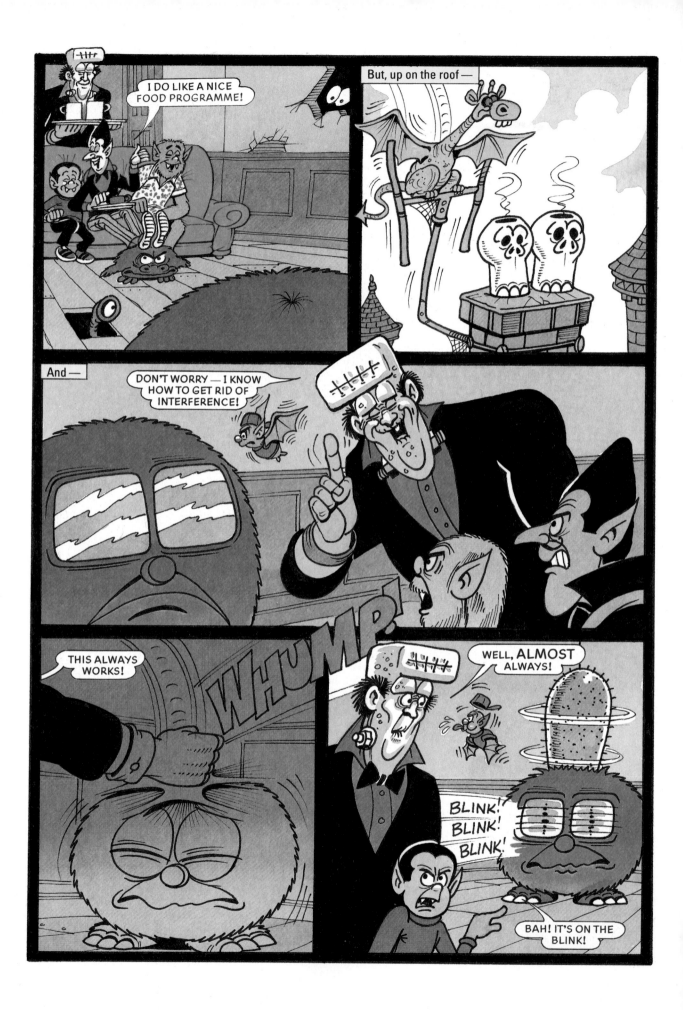

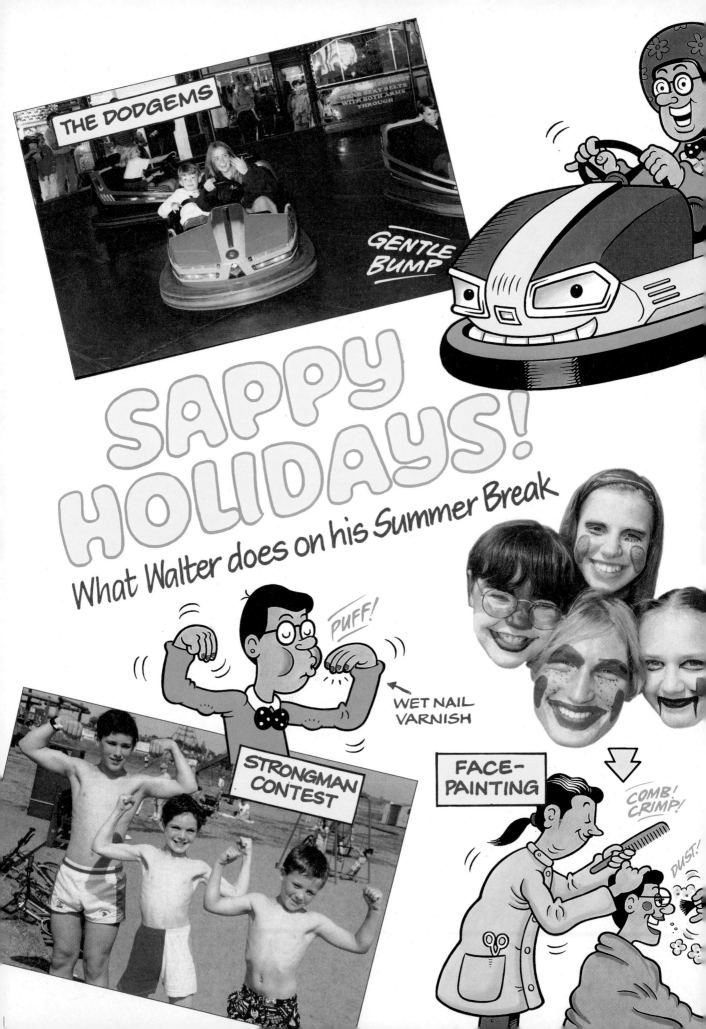

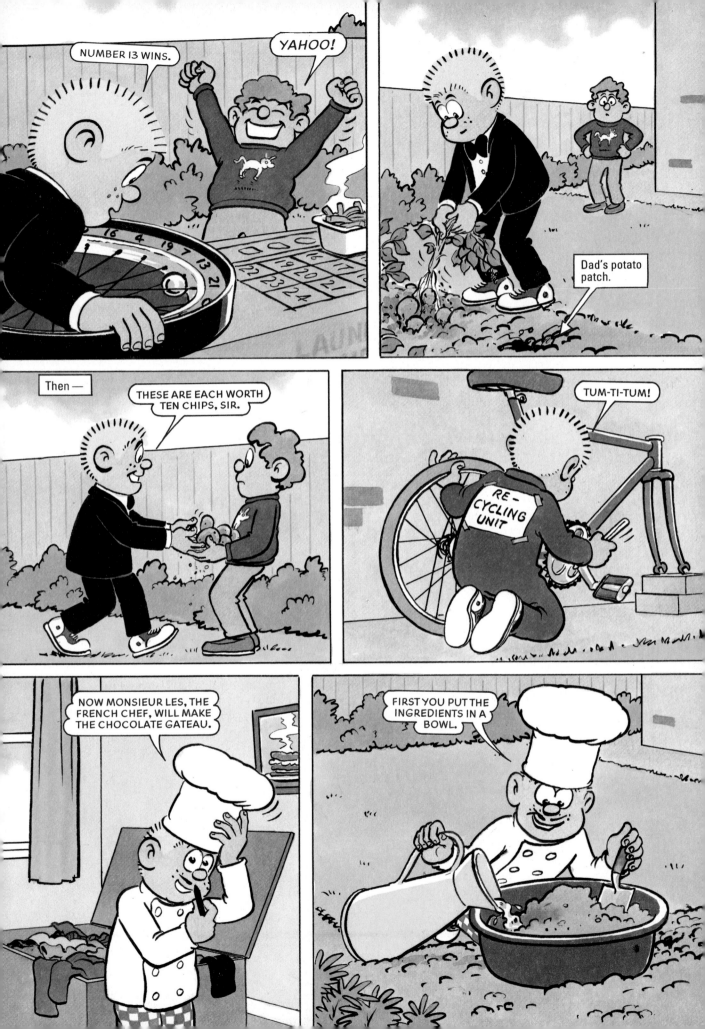

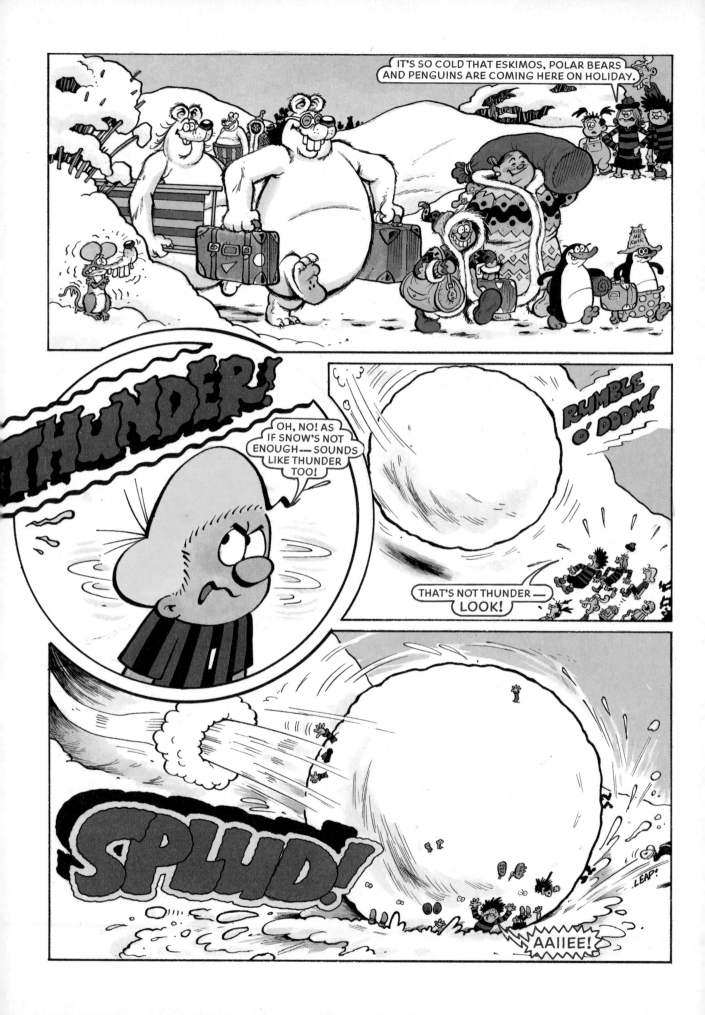

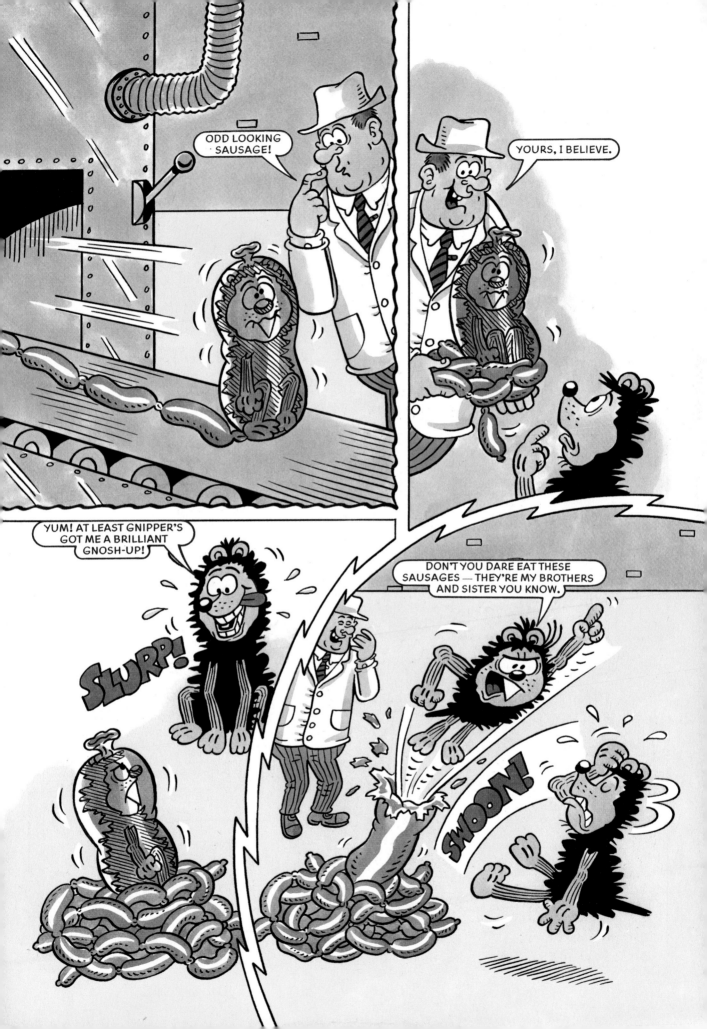

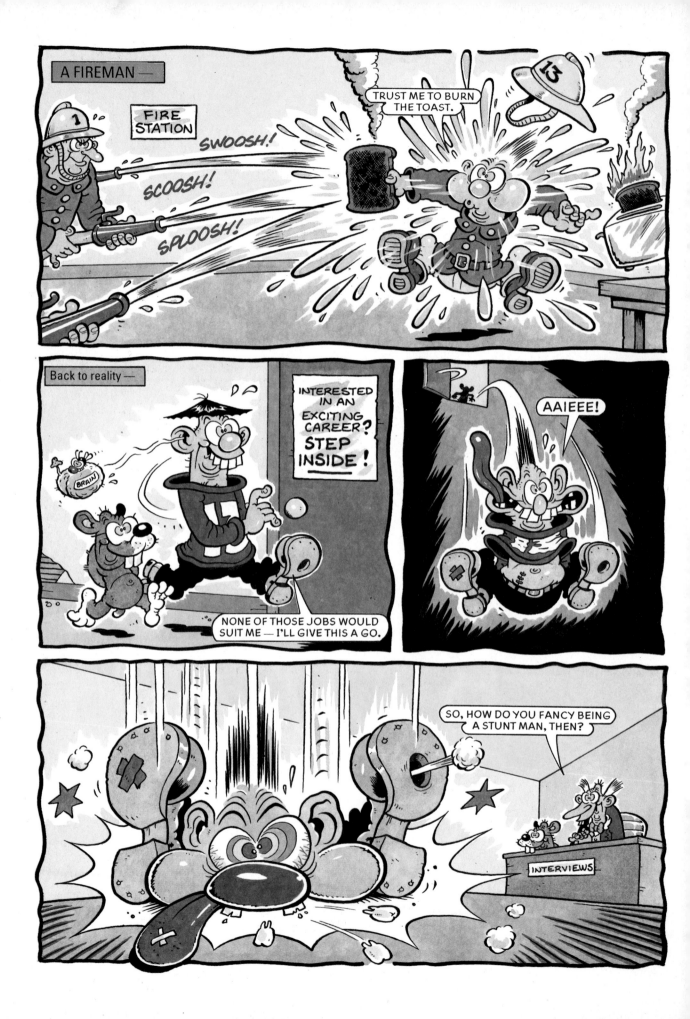

Fun loving redhead interested in meeting a boy into kick boxing, alligator wrestling and Dad Baiting. Will meet you outside the Ballet School. I'll be the one carrying the rotten fruit.

ALL THEY NEED IS ♥ LOVE

CAN YOU GUESS WHICH BEANO CHARACTERS ARE BEHIND THESE LONELY HEART MESSAGES?

Answers over the page.

Night time guy seeks girl to go out with for a bite. Meet me at the graveyard at midnight then we can get together with a few old friends.

Mature woman seeks companion for romantic meals. Once you've tasted my home cooking you'll fall head over heels for me.

LIKE A MAN IN A UNIFORM? THEN LET ME SWEEP YOU OFF YOUR FEET. I'M ALSO VERY FOND OF CHILDREN - - - - 500 MILES AWAY!

I'm a guy with long black hair, a sparkling smile and a cold, wet nose. I love long walks in the country and archaeology (digging up old bones). If you'r interested, meet me at the lamp-post in the town square.

Small Sensitive guy seeks girl (among lots of other things) to help him find his way…

Sporty boy would love to meet tall, athletic girl. Must be in control, a good mover, and able to go out on a Saturday afternoon.

ENJOY SOME DANGER IN YOUR LIFE? WHY NOT GO OUT WITH ME AND I CAN PROMISE YOU NEVER A DULL MOMENT. I HAVEN'T BEEN LUCKY IN LOVE IN THE PAST (IN FACT I HAVEN'T BEEN LUCKY IN ANYTHING IN THE PAST).

ALL THEY NEED IS LOVE

ANSWERS FROM THE
PREVIOUS PAGE